# Rabbit Moon

## Jean Kim

Arthur A. Levine Books  An Imprint of Scholastic Inc.

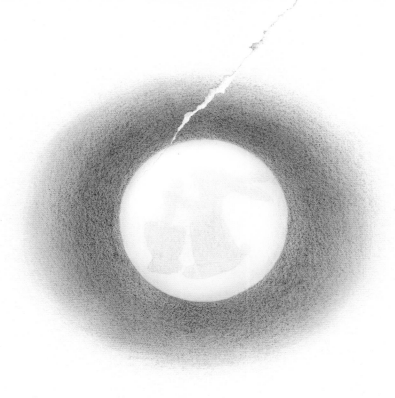

## AUTHOR'S NOTE

What do you see in the moon?
Some people see cheese while others see faces.
Where I'm from, in Korea, when we look at the full moon
we see the outline of a rabbit standing next to a mortar (a kind of
large bowl), pounding rice into rice cakes. When you look up in the sky and
see the rabbit in the moon, it is customary to make a wish, whether it's during the
autumn harvest festival (Chuseok), the first full moon of the Lunar New Year,
or any other full moon throughout the year.

I've always loved this story of hope
and prosperity from Korean folklore, and often
think about all those wishes going up to the sky.
But it makes me wonder: What would the
rabbit in the moon wish for?

A secret dream takes midnight flight.

What is it we wish tonight?

Across the sky . . .

A journey far . . .

Till Rabbit
turns them into
stars.

Wishes fill the sky
with light . . .

. . . twinkling
in the starry night.

Yet Rabbit has his wishes too . . .

# Time for adventure.

Farewell, moon!

But then a POP!

# And a PLOP!

And a friend
to help
Rabbit up.

A warm welcome,
a wish come true!

And with new friends,

so much to do.

Days of play
and fun and light . . .

. . . fade to dark
and peaceful nights.

# But look! The stars!
# Where have they gone?

Rabbit knows what must be done.

Farewell, friends . . .

. . . it's time
to go home.

On Rabbit Moon, there's work
to be done.

And then, across
the brightening sky . . .

One more wish.

# A sweet surprise!

To my parents, who raised me to believe in my dream and encouraged me to go on this adventure.
And to all the lonely rabbits out there.

• Library of Congress Cataloging-in-Publication Data • Names: Kim, Jean (Children's author), author. • Title: Rabbit moon / Jean Kim. • Description: First edition. | New York, NY : Arthur A. Levine Books, an imprint of Scholastic Inc., 2018. | Summary: In rhyming text, Rabbit comes out to play with his friends in the moonlight. • Identifiers: LCCN 2017021063 | ISBN 9781338036398 (hardcover : alk. paper) • Subjects: LCSH: Rabbits—Juvenile fiction. | Friendship—Juvenile fiction. | Night—Juvenile fiction. | Stories in rhyme. | CYAC: Stories in rhyme. | Rabbits—Fiction. | Friendship—Fiction. | Night—Fiction. | LCGFT: Stories in rhyme. Classification: LCC PZ8.3.K5592 Rab 2018 | DDC [E]—dc23 LC record available at https://lccn.loc.gov/2017021063 ISBN 978-1-338-03639-8 • 10 9 8 7 6 5 4 3 2 1          18 19 20 21 22 Printed in China 38 • First edition, February 2018 • The text was set in Tw Cen MT Regular. • The display type was set in Tw Cen MT Regular. • The art for this book was made with pencils and colored in Adobe Photoshop. • Art direction and book design by Marijka Kostiw